Mark Riddle

MARGARASH

Illustrated by
Tim Miller

ENCHANTED LION BOOKS
NEW YORK

More than his telescope, his trains, or his Tyrannosaurus, Collin loved coins.

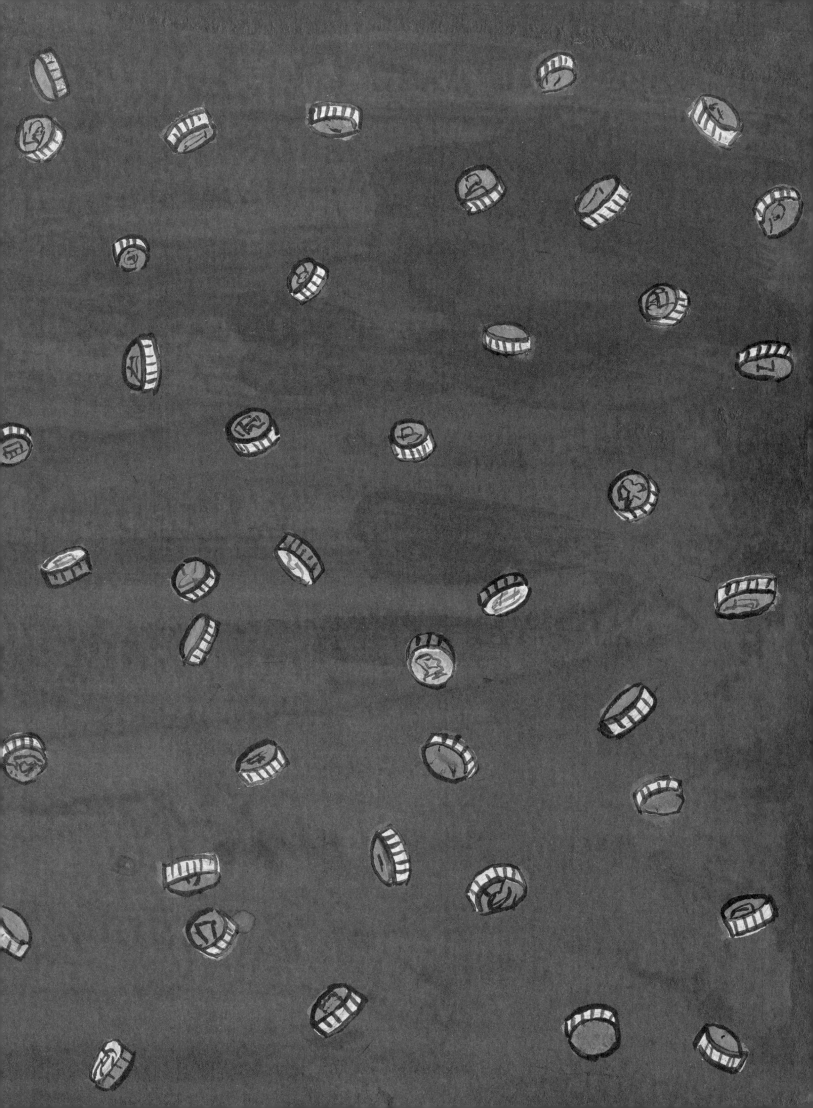

Mark Riddle is a Youth Services Librarian with a colossal beard. He lives in North Carolina with his wife Kate, their cat Warda, and several chickens. As well as writing picture books, he enjoys performing folktales about dragons, frogs and crows as a story-teller. He would love it if you visited www.marktellstales.com. This is Mark's first book.

Tim Miller is the illustrator of *Snappsy the Alligator (Did Not Ask to Be in This Book)* and *Hamstersaurus Rex*. His debut picture book as author and illustrator, *Moo Moo in a Tutu*, will be published in early 2017. Tim studied at the School of Visual Arts where he earned his Bachelor's in Cartooning and his Master's in Art Education. He lives in New York City. You can see more of his work at www.timmillerillustration.com

MARGARASH

For Mike and Marie. — M.R.

For Jose. — T.M.

www.enchantedlion.com

First edition, published in 2016 by Enchanted Lion Books,
351 Van Brunt Street, Brooklyn, NY 11231

Text copyright © 2016 by Mark Riddle
Illustrations copyright © 2016 by Tim Miller
Design & layout: Jonathan Yamakami

A CIP record is on file with the Library of Congress.

ISBN 978-1-59270-216-9

Printed in China by RR Donnelley Asia Printing Solutions Ltd.

1 3 5 7 9 10 8 6 4 2

Curled up on the carpet, Collin arranged them by size or shape, country or state, even by smell or taste (which is something you should never do).

His favorite coin, which was always in his pocket, was a magic coin that turned from a silver quarter into a golden dollar, if you knew the trick.

Collin looked for coins everywhere, but he always found his best
ones deep inside couches, where they'd been lost.

Searching those forgotten spaces could be dangerous, though...
Very, very dangerous, because...

Down...

Down...

Down, in the deep, dark cave that lies below the cushions
and springs of your couch, dwells MARGARASH.

Collin always made fun of this monster legend.

Until the day when he thrust his hand
deep into his parents' couch...

And a scaly hand seized his wrist,
pulling him ferociously into the gap.

Down and around, around and down Collin went, as a hoarse voice sang:

"The coins that fall are for Margarash,
Margarash, Margarash,
The coins that fall are for Margarash,
Leave them where they lie."

In the dust and dirt at the bottom of the spring, the monster grabbed Collin and dragged him off in the direction of an impossibly huge coin pile.

As Margarash stomped ahead with Collin, he scooped up knives, forks, pens, and remote controls that had fallen into his world.

Then he fashioned those into a crude cage.

When he was done, he threw Collin inside.

Collin was sadder than he had ever been. Alone in the dust, he
stared up at the tiny points of light that shone between the cracks
in the couches, shining like dirty stars in a dark sky.

Each day Collin was alone for what seemed like ages, but then Margarash would return from the world above, singing—no, **GROWLING**:

"The coins that fall are for Margarash,
Margarash, Margarash,
The coins that fall are for Margarash,
Leave them where they lie."

And each day, Collin would beg the beast to take him home, but the monster never seemed to hear him. So Collin soon stopped saying anything at all.

Except for when Margarash sat, thoughtful on the ground, arranging his coins. Then Collin would look on in awe as Margarash polished each coin and added it to his collection.

Eventually, whenever Margarash placed a coin where Collin didn't think it should go, he would call out in frustration, unable to stay silent any longer.

"Put that penny over there, it's—"

And each time an **IMMENSE ROAR** would interrupt Collin, who'd leap, terrified, to the back of the cage.

But later, Collin would see Margarash surreptitiously move the penny, the dime, or the half-dollar to the place he had suggested.

And so Collin began to wait for Margarash and his new coins at the end of each day.

And each night, Margarash would roar at Collin, but later would do as he had suggested.

Collin couldn't help but give a little smile when this happened—a teeny tiny smile that he kept to himself.

Still, Collin remained utterly miserable. He missed his telescope, his trains, and his Tyrannosaurus.

Above all, he missed his family.

This might have gone on forever, and Collin might be down there still, had Margarash not seen Collin playing with his magic coin, flicking it from a quarter into a dollar and back again.

In all his centuries, Margarash had never wanted a coin so badly.

"NO!"

Collin shouted, "It's mine!"

"GIVE IT TO ME!" Margarash bellowed back.
"I want that... MAGNIFICENT COIN!"

All at once, a daring idea, a risky idea, a MAGNIFICENT IDEA bloomed in Collin's mind.

He passed the coin to the monster, who stared at it greedily.

Margarash tossed the coin high into the air and watched it fall back into his palm.

But the coin hadn't changed.

"That's strange," Collin said. "You must be doing something wrong. Let me out so I can see better."

A look of suspicion passed briefly over Margarash's face, but he wanted the coin's secret so badly that he unlocked the cage.

Collin watched Margarash try again and again...

But without Collin's secret flick, the quarter remained a quarter.

"I don't know," Collin said, scratching his head. "It always worked for me when I was in the cage..."

Margarash clambered into the cage to test it, but as soon as he crossed the threshold...

Collin slammed the door shut.
The monster clenched his fearsome teeth and stared furiously at Collin.

He rumbled. He roared. He thrashed.
But the cage he had made was strong.

Collin stood back, terrified—by the noise, the monster's flailing
claws, the terrible anger...

But just as he was about to flee, Collin realized that Margarash couldn't harm him. So he watched and waited. And like a thunderstorm breaking up the night sky before disappearing out to sea, Margarash's anger flared up and then left him.

After a time, Margarash said in a slow whisper, "I may be trapped in this cage, but you... you are trapped in *my* world with me."

The monster was right. Collin knew he couldn't climb the couch springs. He didn't even know which couch-star was his own. But he knew one thing Margarash didn't.

"I might stay down here so long that I grow a beard," Collin said. "So long that my hair falls out. I might even lose all of my teeth, and I still won't be able to escape. But you—you'll never get the coin to work. Its magic will only be yours if you take me home."

Margarash growled, muttered, and growled some more. Finally, he said, "You would give up your magic to me? Why?"

"For my family," Collin said simply, and he held out his hand for the coin.

Suspicious, but hungry for the secret, Margarash agreed to the trade.

And so he took Collin and carried him back up the couch spring towards home.

Just as they got there, Collin taught Margarash the secret flick of
the wrist that would transform the magic coin.

Collin pulled himself up out of the couch and flew into his parents' arms.

After a big meal and a long bath, and feeling like the luckiest boy who had ever lived, Collin went to his warm, comfy, safe bed.

But that night, Collin lay awake for hours, unable to sleep without Margarash's nighttime visit.

He wondered what Margarash was doing, what coins he had found.

As for the monster, he sat beside his hoard, bigger and better than ever, but somehow, despite the magic coin clasped tight in his hand, he couldn't decide where to place his newest treasures. For the first time, his realm seemed truly empty.

Early the next morning, Collin tiptoed out from his room to the couch, and there on a scrap of paper, he found a note.

The coins that fall are for Margarash, Margarash, Margarash
The coins that fall are for Margarash
But could be for Collin too!!!!

Collin couldn't help but smile. And this time, it was a big, huge, happy smile, and there was no reason to hide it.

So now, if you put your ear carefully to your couch, you might hear Collin on one of his visits to the couch-cave world, where he and Margarash play with his telescope, trains, and Tyrannosaurus, while stacking and restacking the impossibly huge coin pile and singing:

"The coins that fall are for you and me,
You and me, you and me,
The coins that fall are for you and me,
And this is where they go!"